# Jungle BuLLiEs

by
**Steven Kroll**

*illustrated by*
**Vincent Nguyen**

Marshall Cavendish Children

**O**ne morning Elephant went down to the pond for his bath. But who was there first? Hippo, and he was taking up a lot of space.

Elephant glared at Hippo.

"Get out of the water, Hippo," he said. "I want to bathe in peace."

Elephant was bigger than Hippo, so Hippo splashed out of the pond. But who was lying on the path?

Lion, and he was in the way.

Hippo nudged Lion with his snout.

"Move over, Lion," he said. "I need to get by you." Hippo was bigger than Lion, so Lion ran into the tall grass. But who was sleeping in his favorite spot?

Leopard, and he was snoring loudly.
Lion glared at him.

"Get moving, Leopard," he said. "I want this space for *my* nap."

Lion was bigger than Leopard, so Leopard ran to a nearby tree. But who was sitting in the branches?

Monkey, and he was enjoying the cool breeze.

Leopard glowered at Monkey.

"Get off this branch, Monkey," he said.

Leopard was bigger and fiercer than Monkey, so
Monkey ran away to another tree.

But who did he find there?

His mama! He jumped into her arms.

"Mama," said Monkey, "Leopard is bullying me. He kicked me out of my tree."

Mama replied, "Son, you have to stand up to bullies. You go back to Leopard, and you tell him there's enough room for two on that branch."

But Monkey was still scared.

"He's big," said Monkey, "and he wants that branch all to himself."

"Then I'll go with you," said Mama.

When Leopard saw the monkeys coming, his tail twitched nervously.

Mama whispered some words in Monkey's ear.

Monkey took a deep breath.

Then he said to Leopard, "Don't you tell me what to do, this tree's big enough for two. Share it with me as a friend, don't be mean to me again."

Leopard looked at Monkey. He looked at Mama. "Okay, you can stay," he said.

He turned around, and Monkey and Mama moved closer.

As they sat, Leopard could see Lion sleeping in the tall grass. He thought about how Lion had taken his napping spot. He thought about Monkey's words. He got an idea.

Leopard whispered in Mama's ear.

Then they all jumped down and ran over to Lion.

Leopard took a deep breath.

"Don't you tell me what to do, this spot's big enough for two. Share it with me as a friend, don't be mean to me again."

Lion looked at Leopard. He looked at the monkeys.

"Okay, you can stay," he said.

He moved over, and Leopard and the others joined him. Then Lion saw Hippo on the path. He thought about how Hippo had made him move. He thought about Leopard's words. He got an idea.

Lion whispered in Leopard's ear.

Then Lion, Leopard, Monkey, and Mama ran over to Hippo.

Lion took a deep breath.

"Don't you tell me what to do, this path's big enough for two. Share it with me as a friend, don't be mean to me again."

Hippo looked at Lion. He looked at the other animals.

"Okay, you can stay," he said.

Lion and the others joined him. Then Hippo saw Elephant in the distance. He thought about how Elephant had made him get out of the water. He thought about Lion's words. He got an idea.

Hippo whispered in Lion's ear.

Then Hippo, Lion, Leopard, Monkey, and Mama scowled at Elephant.

Hippo took a deep breath.

"Don't you tell me what to do, this pond's big enough for two. Share it with me as a friend, don't be mean to me again."

Elephant looked at Hippo. He looked at the other animals.

"Come on in!" he said.

Hippo plunged into the water.

Soon he and Elephant were chasing each other.

"This is fun," said Elephant.

"This *is* fun," said Hippo.

Lion, Leopard, Monkey, and Mama joined in, too. And they all said, "Big or little, large or small, this pond's big enough for all. Bullies aren't ever fair, it's a lot more fun to share!"

For Kathleen
—S.K.


For Mom and Dad
—V.N.

Marshall Cavendish Corporation, 99 White Plains Road, Tarrytown, NY 10591
www.marshallcavendish.us/kids

Library of Congress Cataloging-in-Publication Data
Kroll, Steven.
Jungle bullies / by Steven Kroll ; illustrated by Vincent Nguyen.
p. cm.
Summary: To get what they want, the larger jungle animals bully the smaller ones until Mama Monkey shows them
all the benefits of sharing.
ISBN 978-0-7614-5297-3 (hardcover)
ISBN 978-0-7614-5620-9 (paperback)
[1. Bullies—Fiction. 2. Sharing—Fiction. 3. Jungle animals—Fiction. 4. Animals—Fiction.] I. Nguyen, Vincent, ill. II. Title.
PZ7.K9225Jun 2006
[E]—dc22
2005027072

*The illustrations are rendered in watercolor, charcoal pencil, and digital techniques.*
*Book design by Symon Chow*

Printed in Malaysia (T)
1 3 5 6 4 2

7/11

**DATE DUE**

| | | | |
|---|---|---|---|
| AUG 0 2 | | | |
| AUG 1 8 | | | |
| OCT 0 7 | | | |
| OCT 1 3 | | | |
| DEC 0 1 | | | |
| APR 0 2 | | | |
| APR 1 2 | | | |
| DEC 0 4 2013 | | | |
| | | | |
| | | | |
| | | | |
| | | | |
| | | | |
| | | | |
| | | | |
| | | | |
| | | | |

DEMCO 38-296

# The Tale of Napkin

# RABBIT

*Written by* A. J. WOOD

*Illustrated by* MAGGIE DOWNER

AN ARTISTS & WRITERS GUILD BOOK
Golden Books
Western Publishing Company, Inc.
850 Third Avenue, New York, N.Y. 10022

Produced and devised by The Templar Company plc.
Designed by Mike Jolley and Janie Louise Hunt.
Napkin Rabbit designed by Paul Jackson.

Printed and bound in Singapore.

Library of Congress Catalog Card Number:
93-9864
A MCMXCIII

ISBN: 0-307-17603-7

Milly was bored. It was raining too hard to play outside, and there was no one to play with indoors. Her brother, Hugo, wouldn't play with her. He was pretending to be an explorer on his way to the North Pole.

"You can't come, 'cause there weren't any girls there," he explained impatiently.

"There weren't any mice, either!" said Milly, pointing to the white pet mouse that was peeping out from under Hugo's collar.

Milly's mother spoke up. "Why don't you have a tea party for your toys?" she suggested.

"I had one yesterday," Milly complained. She looked across the room. Her toys were still sitting around their shoebox table— Captain Penguin, Teddy, Stripey Clown, Green Monkey, and Lucy Doll. "They don't want tea today."

"Well, never mind," said Milly's mother. "Your Uncle George will be here in a little while. He'll find something for you to do."

The thought of Uncle George coming cheered Milly up. She loved it when he came to dinner. He was old and had had lots of adventures. He could even do magic tricks.

When Uncle George finally arrived, he asked Milly what she would most like to do.

"I would like to go on an expedition into the jungle with Bibsy and Bobsy," she answered, pointing out to the rainy yard where her pet rabbits lived. "But it's too wet to play outdoors, and we're not allowed to bring our pets inside," Milly said, staring at her brother.

"What you need is an *indoor* rabbit," said Uncle George. "Lucky for you, I know just how to make one. Pass me your napkin, please."

Milly watched as Uncle George quickly folded her napkin this way and that. Before long the head of a rabbit appeared. Then Uncle George took another napkin from the second drawer of the sideboard and made a rabbit's body. He put the two together and—Napkin Rabbit was born.

Milly squealed with delight as Uncle George took out his big black fountain pen and drew a black nose and beady eyes on Napkin Rabbit.

"You could sew on some black whiskers if you like," said Uncle George. "There, he's all yours!"

Milly loved Napkin Rabbit. He wasn't like her other toys. His ears were all floppy, and he looked kind of lonely. Milly decided to cheer him up. She introduced him to Hugo (who was at that very moment being attacked by a polar bear) and to Hugo's mouse (who had hidden in the sideboard). Then she introduced Napkin Rabbit to her other toys. When they saw him, Lucy Doll screwed up her nose and Teddy growled, but Milly did not notice.

That night Milly made a special shoebox bed for Napkin Rabbit. It had a soft sock pillow and a kitchen towel blanket. Milly tucked Napkin Rabbit in and wished him good night. Then she put him in the toy cupboard with the other toys and went to bed.

As soon as the doors shut, Napkin Rabbit could hear the other toys start to talk. He strained his floppy white ears to hear what was being said.

"Fancy being tucked in bed like a baby," said Captain Penguin. In fact, he was jealous, since he had once had a shoebox bed himself.

"Pooh!" said Teddy. "I don't know what all the fuss is about. After all, he's not even a real toy. He's made out of *napkins*!"

"Napkins?" said Lucy Doll. "How common! He's certainly not one of us."

Poor Napkin Rabbit. He lay in his shoebox feeling thoroughly miserable. None of the toys liked him, and he couldn't really blame them.

He *wasn't* a proper toy like they were.
He belonged in the second drawer
of the sideboard, an ordinary
napkin like all the rest.

The next morning, sunshine streamed into the toy cupboard when Milly opened the doors. It was a beautiful day.

"Good morning, toys," Milly cried happily. "Good morning, Napkin Rabbit!"

"Huh!" Teddy muttered crossly. "Why does *he* get a special 'Good morning'?"

Milly lifted Napkin Rabbit out of his shoebox bed and set him down gently on the windowsill.

"Now, you stay there while I eat my breakfast," she said, settling down at the table. She unfolded a big blue napkin and tucked it under her chin. Napkin Rabbit glanced at the other toys. They were all looking out of the cupboard. They looked at Milly and her big blue breakfast napkin. Then they looked at him. Napkin Rabbit shuddered. He knew just what they were thinking.

Even if the toys didn't like him, Milly certainly did. She played with Napkin Rabbit all that day and all the next. She took him with her when she went in the car with her mother (which was terribly exciting) and when she played outside.

She even took him to bed with her, but she rolled over and squashed him a bit in the night.

"Poor Napkin Rabbit!" Milly said the next morning as she plumped up his ears. "You've almost come unfolded!"

UNFOLDED! Napkin Rabbit shuddered and shook. What a terrible thought! If he was unfolded, he would be just an ordinary napkin again, shut away in the second drawer of the sideboard. He was glad when Milly straightened his folds.

However, when he looked
around, he saw that the
other toys were staring
at him again, and
some of them were
smiling in a strange way.

That night Milly put Napkin Rabbit back in his shoebox bed. "You'll be safe here," she said, stroking his floppy white ears. But as soon as she closed the cupboard doors, Napkin Rabbit could hear the other toys whispering in the darkness, whispering his name.

Poor creature! He knew the other toys didn't like him. Maybe they were planning to get rid of him. Maybe they would try to unfold him!

All the next day Napkin Rabbit felt frightened. He tried again and again to tell Milly what was wrong, but she couldn't hear him. Then it began to get dark. Napkin Rabbit knew he would soon be put back into the cupboard with horrid Lucy Doll and the others.

"Surely they won't unfold me!" Napkin Rabbit said to himself. But he could tell from the glint in Teddy's eyes what the toys were planning, and there was nothing he could do to stop them. Or was there?

Now, Napkin Rabbit wasn't the cleverest rabbit in the world, but the same magic that allowed him to walk and talk also allowed him to think. And suddenly a thought came into his head.

"Run away!" said the thought. It was a terrifying prospect, but Napkin Rabbit knew that was exactly what he had to do. Seconds later, while Milly wasn't looking, Napkin Rabbit slipped out through the open window and down into the darkness of the summer garden. . . .

When Milly came to put Napkin Rabbit to bed, she was surprised to find the windowsill empty.

"I'm sure I left him here," she said. "Did you take him, Hugo?" Her brother hadn't seen him and neither had Mommy. "Where can he be?" cried Milly, and she wept all the way to bed.

In the toy cupboard Lucy Doll and Teddy were enjoying the news.

"He's run away," crowed Lucy Doll. "We're rid of him after all."

"Good riddance," said Captain Penguin. "But I wish Milly wasn't so upset."

"Oh, she'll be all right tomorrow," said Teddy. "We can have a tea party to cheer her up."

But Milly wasn't all right the next day, and they didn't have a tea party. In fact, Milly didn't play with them at all. Instead, she searched the house from top to bottom looking for Napkin Rabbit. When she couldn't find him, she sat on the window seat and cried.

Now, I suppose you are wondering how Napkin Rabbit was doing. Well, at first he was frightened by the dark garden. He couldn't see where he was going, and there were strange noises all around him.

He had just started to cross the great expanse of lawn when he bumped into one of the noises. It was a small green frog whose name was Lawrence.

"You want to be careful out here," Lawrence warned. "There are owls and cats and other things that would like to eat you up."

"I don't think I'd be very tasty," said Napkin Rabbit. "I'm only made of napkins. Actually, that's my problem." And he told Lawrence all about his escape from the nursery.

"What you need is a hideout," said Lawrence, sounding very sure of himself. "I know just the place. You may not be a real rabbit, but you're a rabbit of sorts, so follow me."

Across the garden they went, Lawrence the frog and Napkin Rabbit, past the flowering border, where Milly's mother grew carnations; past the ornamental fishpond, where Lawrence lived under a stone; and into a dark garden shed. Then Lawrence stopped. Above him was a box with wire netting over the front.

"Is anybody at home?" Lawrence croaked. Seconds later two quivering noses appeared at the wire, and two pairs of beady brown eyes, as well as the longest, whitest whiskers Napkin Rabbit had ever seen. It was Bibsy and Bobsy, Milly's pet rabbits.

Now, Napkin Rabbit had never seen a *real* rabbit before, and he was overjoyed. When Bibsy and Bobsy heard his story, they were most sympathetic and invited him to stay for as long as he liked. So, with a little help from Lawrence (who was very good with latches), Napkin Rabbit squeezed inside the cage.

Before long he was fast asleep in a pile of straw. It had been a very tiring day.

The next day Napkin Rabbit stayed in the cage with Bibsy and Bobsy. They fed him dandelions and pieces of carrot (which were very flavorsome indeed) and told him about themselves . . . how they had lived in a pet shop next to a horrid hamster until Milly's father bought them for Milly's sixth birthday.

Later in the morning Lawrence came to visit. "You will have to hide soon," he warned Napkin Rabbit. "I've just heard Hugo complaining that he has to feed Bibsy and Bobsy today because Milly can't do it."

Sure enough, at the house all was not well. Milly was so upset about Napkin Rabbit's disappearance that she had gone to bed. The toys were beginning to regret what they had done.

"We shouldn't have been so horrid," Captain Penguin told Lucy Doll. "He was only made from napkins, but he was a toy just like us."

"I agree," said Teddy. "And now we've upset Milly, and that wasn't the plan."

"Oh, all right!" said Lucy Doll crossly. "We made a mistake. But what can we do to set things right? Goodness knows where that rabbit is by now."

There was silence in the toy cupboard until Green Monkey swung down to offer an idea. "Why don't you ask Thomas?" he said.

Now, Thomas was the cat that belonged to Milly's mother. He didn't usually talk to the toys, being a superior sort of animal. But he knew everything about everything, so the toys agreed to go to him.

"Of course I know where he is," Thomas answered lazily when questioned. "Everyone is talking about it in the garden."

"Will you take us to him?" Teddy pleaded. "We want to ask him to come back."

"Well, if it's for Milly . . ." said Thomas.

That night the toys waited anxiously for darkness to fall. As soon as a bright silver moon appeared through the nursery window, they climbed up onto Thomas's back and set off for the garden shed.

Napkin Rabbit was most surprised to see the toys—and afraid that they had come to unfold him after all.

"No, no!" said Captain Penguin in dismay. "We want you to come home. Milly is unhappy, and it's all our fault. Won't you please come back—and be our friend?"

Well, how could Napkin Rabbit refuse? He was getting rather tired of carrots and dandelions anyway. He thanked the rabbits for their help, and then back they all went with Thomas, back across the moon-bright lawn, into the sleeping house, and back to the safety of the toy cupboard at last.

Napkin Rabbit lay down gratefully in his shoebox bed and thought about his remarkable adventure. He had promised to visit Bibsy and Bobsy whenever he could, and Lawrence as well. The toys were all being nice to him, and Captain Penguin wanted to be his best friend.

Lucky Napkin Rabbit!

Having had no friends at all,
he suddenly had more
than he could count.

The one who loved Napkin Rabbit the best, however, didn't know he was back—until she opened the toy cupboard the next morning.

"Napkin Rabbit!" Milly cried when she saw him. "Wherever have you been?" Milly never did find out, because no one ever told her. It was the toys' secret, and a secret it would stay.

# NAPKIN RABBIT

**Remember:**

Ask a grown-up to starch and iron your napkins before you start.

Always run your thumbnail down each fold to give a nice crisp crease.

Practice making some rabbits out of paper napkins before you start on your cotton one.

**You will need:**

Two napkins; a stick of glue or a needle and white thread; a black felt-tip pen; some old stockings.

## Head

**1.** Fold the top and bottom edges of your first napkin to the center.

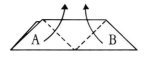

**2.** Fold in the corners and then fold in half as shown.

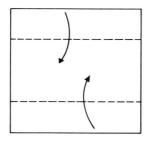

**3.** Fold A and B upward, like this.

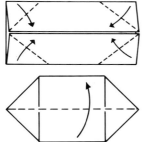

Now fold C and D into the middle.

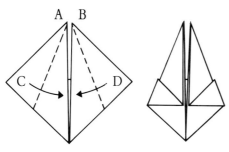

**4.** Turn the napkin over and turn up the nose.

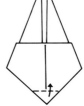

**5.** Fold in half down the middle. The head is now complete. Hold together with a paper clip while you make the body.

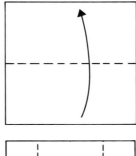

## Body

**6.** Fold your second napkin in half. Then fold the sides to the middle. Unfold them again.

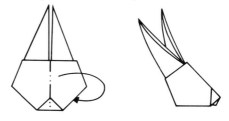

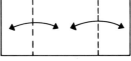

**7.** Fold in the corners.

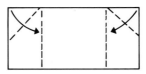

Then fold the sides to the middle.

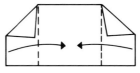

**8.** Fold up the bottom edge to the center.

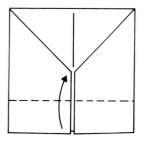

**9.** Pull down A and B, like this. Fold in half.

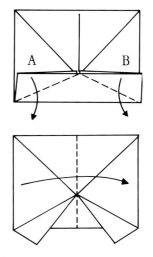

**10.** Fold corner C back and forth.

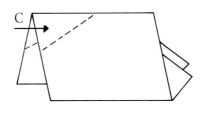

**11.** Make a second creaseline at C inside the original line.

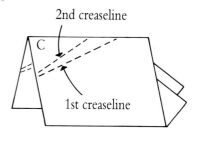

**12.** Open the body. Push corner C inside the body along the first creaseline . . . like this:

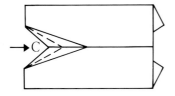

**13.** Holding the body at D, pull out C along the second creaseline to make the tail. Now fold in the bottom corners. The body is now complete.

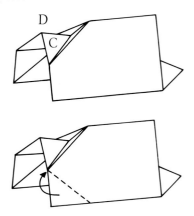

**Assembly**

**14.** Use your stick of glue or your needle and white cotton thread to attach the head to the body and also to secure the folds where shown (marked with ★ on the diagram below).
Use your felt-tip pen to draw on Napkin Rabbit's eyes and nose. You could rethread your needle with black cotton thread and give him whiskers, too! Finally, fill his body with tissues or a piece of old stocking to give him a good shape.